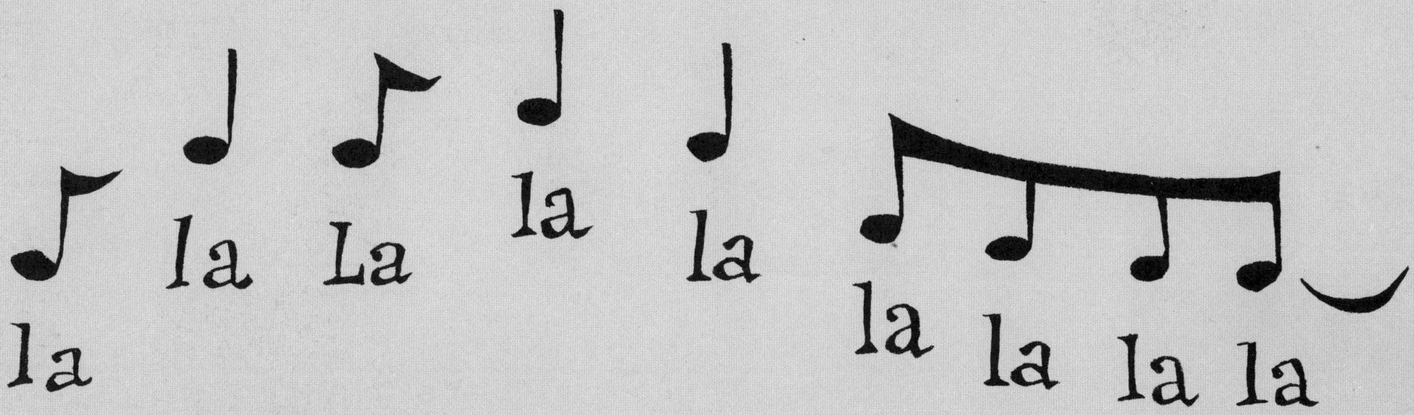
la
la
La
la
la
la
la
la
la

Lyrics and Music by Joe Raposo

Story in Pictures by Tom Lichtenheld

Christy Ottaviano Books

HENRY HOLT AND COMPANY · NEW YORK

Sing,

Sing a song.

Sing out loud,

sing out strong.

Sing of
good things,
not bad.

Sing of
happy,
not sad.

Sing,

sing a song.

Make it simple

to last your whole life long.

Don't worry that
it's not good enough
for anyone else to hear.

Just sing,

Sing a song!

SING!

Words and Music by Joe Raposo

Sing!
Sing a song
Sing out loud
Sing out strong

Sing of good things, not bad
Sing of happy, not sad

Sing!
Sing a song
Make it simple
To last your whole life long

Don't worry that it's not good enough
For anyone else to hear

Sing!
Sing a song

the end

La-la-la-la-la La-la-la-la-la-la La-la-la-la-la-la
La-la-la-la-la La-la-la-la-la-la La-la-la-la-la-la

Canta
Canta una canción
Canta en voz alta
Canta fuerte
Cosas buenas, no malos
Alegre, no triste
Canta
Canta una canción
Make it simple to last your whole life long (Todo la vida)
Don't worry that it's not good enough for anyone else to
hear
Canta
Canta una canción

La-la-la-la-la La-la-la-la-la-la La-la-la-la-la-la-la
La-la-la-la-la La-la-la-la-la-la La-la-la-la-la-la-la

el extremo

(Spanish translation by Andrew Belcher)

Sing

Sing a song

~~out loud~~
Sing ~~it pretty~~

Sing out strong
~~Not long~~

~~Make~~ Sing of good things
~~Sing a song of good~~

not bad –

~~Make~~ Sing of happy
~~Sing a song of happy~~

~~not sad~~ – not sad

Sing

Sing a song

Make it simple
~~Sing~~
~~Make it good~~

To last your whole life long
(D   E E   J   C   D
Don't ~~worry~~ ~~like~~ that it's not
        E
        good enough
D   E E D
For ~~anyone~~ C   B   A
~~Sing~~ ~~anybody~~ else to hear
Sing a Song – ~~~~

A Note about "Sing!" from Nick Raposo

MY FATHER loved "Sing!" It has been translated into thirty-five languages and remains one of the world's most recorded children's songs. My father put himself into every song he wrote, but none more so than "Sing!" Coming from a Portuguese immigrant household where English was his second language, my father felt silenced and excluded in America in the 1940s. By 1971, he'd graduated from Harvard and the École Normale Supérieure in Paris and knew that no one should be silenced based on ethnicity, language, or social class. Asked to write a bilingual song about self-acceptance for *Sesame Street*, he penned "Canta-Sing!" Its simple lyrics are a line drawn in the sand against shame and bigotry. He would be overjoyed to know that more than forty years later his message of courage, pride, and hope was still reaching children everywhere.

Joe and Nick Raposo, 1985

Original handwritten lyrics and chords by Joe Raposo circa 1971

To every child, everywhere. Don't worry if it's not good enough: Just sing!
NICK RAPOSO

Thanks to Christy Ottaviano for bringing this special project to me;
to Eric Rohmann and the Crusty Nibs for their priceless input;
and to my wife, Jan, for her love and guidance.
TOM LICHTENHELD

Henry Holt and Company, LLC
Publishers since 1866
175 Fifth Avenue · New York, New York 10010
mackids.com

Henry Holt® is a registered trademark of Henry Holt and Company, LLC.
Music and lyrics copyright © 1971 by Jonico Music, Inc., © renewed 1998, Greenfox Music, Inc. Used by permission
of the Joe Raposo Music Group, Inc. · Illustrations copyright © 2013 by Tom Lichtenheld.
All rights reserved.

Library of Congress Cataloging-in-Publication Data
Raposo, Joe.
Sing! / lyrics and music by Joe Raposo ; story in pictures by Tom Lichtenheld. — First edition.
pages   cm
"Christy Ottaviano Books."
Summary: An illustrated presentation of the classic Sesame Street
song about self-expression and the celebration of music.
ISBN 978-0-8050-9071-0 (hardcover)
1. Children's songs, English—United States—Texts. [1. Singing—Songs and music. 2. Songs.]
I. Lichtenheld, Tom, illustrator. II. Title.
PZ8.3.R1765Si 2013   782.42—dc23   [E]   2012027321

First Edition—2013
The artist used ink, watercolor, pastels, and colored pencil to create the illustrations for this book.
Printed in China by South China Printing Co. Ltd., Dongguan City, Guangdong Province
1 3 5 7 9 10 8 6 4 2

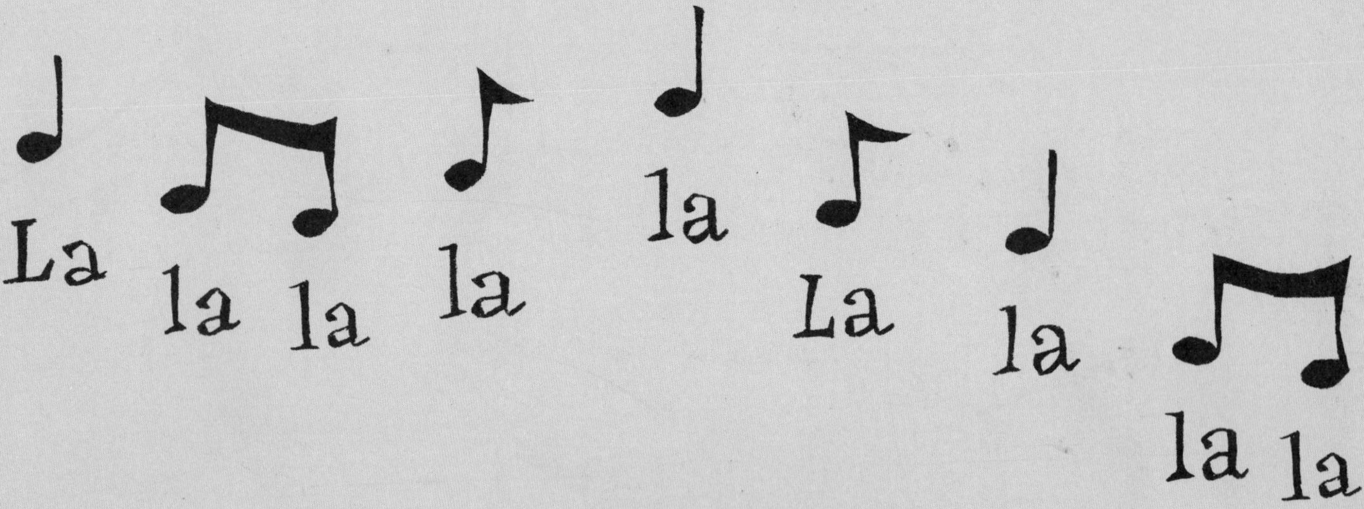
La la la la la La la la la